ELLA

Diaries

TOP SECRET!

For Ella, Alex and Nellie—May all your own
dreams come true!—M.C.

Meredith Costain

For Chelsea, Alyssa and Bonsi. x—D.M.

Danielle M°Donald

First American Edition 2016
Kane Miller, A Division of EDC Publishing

Text copyright © Meredith Costain, 2015
Illustrations copyright © Danielle McDonald, 2015

First published by Scholastic Australia, a division of Scholastic Australia Pty Limited in 2015.
This edition published under license from Scholastic Australia Pty Limited.

Library of Congress Control Number: 2015954253

Printed and bound in the United States of America

7 8 9 10

ISBN: 978-1-61067-523-9

ELLA
Diaries

Dreams
Come
True

Kane Miller
A DIVISION OF EDC PUBLISHING

Wednesday, after school

Dear Diary,

I can't believe it. It can't possibly be true.

But it IS!!!

Cassi Valentine—the best most excellent pop star in the WHOLE WILD WORLD— is coming here. To my town.

Maybe even to MY SCHOOL!!!

ZOW-EE!

I ♥ Cassi Valentine

SOOO MUCH!

✿ 5 ✿

THINGS I ♥ ABOUT CASSI VALENTINE

♥ **1** Her song lyrics.
She writes them all
herself and they are always
about fabulously fabulous
stuff like girl power and
best friends and NEVER
about soppy, lovey-dovey things like
boyfriends and kissing—eww.

2 Her music. It's
super funky and
great to sing along
to when you have
to do boring stuff
like cleaning up your
bedroom. ♫ ♫ ♫ ♫ ♫

GIRL Power

TaLa La...

3 Her dance moves. They make you want to get up and move, move, move even if you are feeling annoyed with someone for "accidentally" borrowing your stuff without asking first (which quite often happens in my house, not that I am naming names or anything— but be warned, if you go running to Mom saying I'm being mean to you again then I will KNOW you have been reading my diary, OLIVIA!!!).

4 Her outfits. These are always SUPER STYLISH (just like mine).

Cassi Valentine is aMAZing!

I have pictures of her
all over the walls of my
bedroom.

And **ALL** of her songs on my MP3 player.

I have the Cassi Valentine lunch box

and drink bottle

and tote bag

and sun visor.

Even my dog, Bob, has a Cassi Valentine bandana. He looks SOOO super stylish in it.

BOB

Bandana

As you can see I am Cassi Valentine's Number One Fan.

Meeting her would be my dream come true.

But wait. It gets EVEN BETTER!

Cassi Valentine's record company is running a competition. Ms. Weiss told us about it in class today. You have to make a video about performing arts* at your school. And the school that creates the best video wins a free lunchtime concert from—guess who!? You got it. CASSI VALENTINE. SINGING LIVE!

* Performing arts means stuff like singing, dancing, music and acting. All the things I am naturally good at.

Ms. Weiss isn't a singing or music teacher—she's just our normal classroom teacher. But she loves all that performing arts stuff. She even said she would help us to make the video if anyone in our class wants to enter.

VIDEO

So then everybody** started waggling their hands in the air and asking a gatrillion questions about the competition. But Ms.  Weiss said we had to keep working hard on our Transportation Through the Ages projects for the rest of the afternoon, and she'd tell us more tomorrow.

That is SO NOT FAIR!

I want to get started right away!

** Well, everybody except (most of) the boys. Boys are SO **BORING**. And Fiona McTavish, who only likes bagpipe music.

Bagpipes! Bleuchhh!

Have to go now, Diary. Dad's calling me to help with dinner.

C u later!

Wednesday night, in bed, very, VERY late

Dear Diary,

Ms. Weiss is **Sooo uhFair** making us wait until tomorrow to find out more about the competition. It is ESSENTIAL that I know ALL the details about it RIGHT NOW.

tick
tock

tick
tock

LIKE:

 1 How many people get to be in the video and

2 Who those people are going to be and

 3 How they will choose them and—most importantly of all—

4 What I'm going to wear when I meet Cassi ☺

If it wasn't so late I could call Zoe so
we could discuss it together. Zoe is
my BFF and very ~~nollagible knolligable~~
clever. She always knows the answer to
EVERYTHING.

Maybe she's even
sitting up in bed
right at this very
moment, thinking
exactly the same
thoughts, and
wanting to call
ME!

But no way would our moms let us talk to each other this late at night. We'd both have to be practically DYING of some terrible, ghastly, vile disease that makes all your teeth and toenails and brains fall out—eww—before they'd let that happen. And maybe not even then. ☹

Guess I'm going to have to wait until tomorrow.

WAAAAAAHHHHHHH!

Good night, DD.

xx

Thursday morning, super early

Dearest Diary,

I just had the weirderest* dream.

Zoe and I were at a big sports stadium
in the city. The stands were packed to the
rafters with millions of screaming fans
waving black and red banners.

And standing on a teeny tiny stage right
in the middle of the stadium was Cassi
Valentine! She was dressed in a super-
stylish outfit and singing my favorite song:

Get up and DANCE.

Then she picked up this bright-red yelling thing like Mr. Floog uses at the swim meets and called out to me with it, like this:

Me! She wanted me! So I jumped out of my seat and raced down to join her on the stage.

Except just as I got there the ground around the stage turned into a moat—like castles had in the olden days—and I had to swim against a raging current and there was this huge spiky pineapple thing blocking my way. Every time I tried to push past it, it poked me in the eye.

PINEAPPLE thing

Moat

What do you think it all means?

* weirderest = weird to the power of 10 million.

Thursday afternoon, after school

Hey, Diary,

Well, there is just SO MUCH to tell you.

We kept bugging Ms. Weiss all morning to tell us more about the Cassi Valentine Video Competition (CVVC). But she just kept smiling and saying annoying things like:

All in good time.

Ms. Weiss

Good things come to those who wait.

It was SO EXASPERATING!

Finally, about five minutes before the lunchtime bell, when we were all just about to go OUT OF OUR MINDS with desperation and run around the room screaming, she told our class to put our Transportation Through the Ages projects away.

Aaarrrgh

So we packed up our
notebooks and pencils
and glitter pens and
construction paper and glue and
scissors and half-finished
drawings of zeppelins and
penny-farthing bicycles and
packhorses and steam trains in
record time.

ZEPPELINS
×

penny-farthing bicycles
×

Then we sat quietly at our desks, with our hands folded neatly and our eyes all shiny and keen, waiting for the good things. (Except for (most of) the boys and Fiona the Bagpipes-Loving Girl, who either stared out the window at random birds or secretly played Battleships.)

Battleships

Ms. Weiss told us there is going to be a meeting about the video next Monday in the music room. And if you want to be involved, you have to come along with your BEST IDEAS about what should be in it.

And she and Mr. Zugaro, who is going to be her helper with the project (YES!!!*), will listen to all the ideas and choose the best one.

* Mr. Zugaro was my teacher last year which means he already knows I am very creative. He told me the poem I wrote called "Ode to a shivering sparrow on a rainy winter's day" was a MASTERPIECE and the best poem he had ever read that week, and that I was obviously a TRUE ARTIST. So he is pretty much 100% sure to pick my idea.

Here is my poem in case you wanted to read it.
WARNING: It is VERY sad.

Ode to a shivering sparrow on a rainy winter's day

Poor little sparrow
I hope you're not in pain
Shiver, shiver, shivering
In the pouring rain

Dear little sparrow
Stuck out in the storm
I wish that I could bring you in
Where it's nice and warm

And then Ms. Weiss asked if
there were any questions.

A forest of arms shot into the air.

This is what happened next. (Unbelievable, I
know. I am STILL outraged to the power of
100.)

Ms. Weiss (pointing to Peach): Yes, Peach?
Me (under my breath): Hmmmmphhh.
(It is SOOO not fair that yucky old Peach

Parker got to ask the first question, ~~exspesh~~ especially as our hands went up at EXACTLY the same time. Now Ms. Weiss will think she is the keenest person out of the whole class, and will probably give her all the best parts in the video.)

Peach (in that sucky, whiny voice she puts on when she's sucking up to teachers, which is ~~most~~ all of the time): First of all, I just wanted to thank you for volunteering your valuable time to help us out with this inspirational, exciting and educational opportunity.

Peach
PARKER

(Sucking UP)

Me: (Silent eye roll at Zoe.)

Zoe: (Silent eye roll back at me.)

Ms. Weiss (looking pleased): Thank you, Peach. That's very sweet of you to think that.

Zoe and me: (Silent gagging motions but done behind our hands in case Ms. Weiss sees us and tells us off for having bad manners.)

Peach (smiling prettily, like sharks do just before they chomp you into little pieces): You're welcome. My question is: is anyone

who wants to allowed to go in the video
or are you just choosing naturally gifted
people with real talent?

(Like her, she means, and her silly friends
Prinny and Jade. Ha! I'll show them what
REAL TALENT is.)

Ms. Weiss: Anyone who would like to be in
the video can be. We're all talented here in
our own special way. But we're going to
need some very special people to do some
of the key things, of course.
Peach (smiling even prettier): Of course.
And Ms. Weiss?
Ms. Weiss: Yes, Peach?

Peach: I have some excellent ideas for the meeting.

Ms. Weiss: Good! I look forward to hearing them. Next?

Peach waited until Ms. Weiss was answering Daisy Tay's next question, then turned around and smirked at me. And so did Prinny and Jade.

Sometimes Peach makes me so mad, I want to SCREAM!!!!

I didn't feel like asking Ms. Weiss any of

my questions after that, even though I had some really excellent ones. So I just sat there feeling morose* until the bell went for lunch.

* Morose means being stuck all alone by yourself without any friends or pets or your MP3 player on a deserted desert island. Oops—I think that word is actually "marooned." But they feel like they mean kind of the same thing. Maybe they're really just the same word but with different spelling??

Signed, your extremely morose, marooned friend,
Ella

Friday afternoon, after school

Dearest Diary,

At lunchtime today, Zoe and I held an

in our special place under the cypress
trees, trying to think up cool ideas for
the video that would be better than
Peach's. Usually when we have Emergency
Meetings we are positively DROWNING
in good ideas and can't write them down
quickly enough. But everything we came up
with seemed dumb to the power of 10.

Princess Perfect Peach had sucked up all our ~~creativerity~~ creativity. And then suddenly, out of nowhere, came a splendidly BRILLIANT IDEA!

We could have a sleepover at my place on Saturday night! And invite all our friends, like Georgia and Poppy and Chloe and Daisy and Cordelia. We can play Cassi's music, and sing along to her video clips, and make up our own dance routines.

Then, once we're
feeling all inspired
and Cassi-fied, we
can settle down in
our sleeping gear, eat
HEAPS of chocolatey
snacks, and think
about ideas for the
meeting on Monday.

It is going to be the BEST SLEEPOVER
EVER!

Now all I have to do is get Mom and Dad to
let me have it.

Wish me luck, Diary! (Because you know what happened at the last sleepover, don't you? Mom is still trying to get the Krazee Kolor pink and purple hair color out of the pillowcases and cushion covers we slept on that night. Personally, I think they look rather stylish. Kind of like the tie-dyed T-shirts my Nanna Kate used to wear back when she was my age, about 900 years ago.)

Nanna KATE

tie-dyed T-Shirt

xox

Friday night, in bed, just before lights-out

Dear Diary,

Guess what! Mom and Dad said yes to our CVVC sleepover!

But only under strict conditions.

SLeepOver ~~STRICT~~ CONDitioNS

1 NO Krazee Kolor hair color or any
   other brand of hair color products ~~aloud~~
allowed.

2 We have to promise that the light goes
   out (and STAYS OUT) at exactly
10:30 pm. Even if we're still all wide-
awake.

tick   tock

3 We have to be respectful of the
   neighbors (and other members
of the family, including Bob) and
not play our music (or squeal) too loudly.

We have to have some
healthy snacks (like fruit
and juice) as well as our sleepover treats.

 Olivia has to be allowed to come or the
whole thing WILL BE CANCELED
WITH NO ARGUMENTS.

Of course I said yes to everything. Even
Condition Number 5. Of course DARLING
Olivia is very welcome to come—just as
long as she sticks to MY strict conditions.

MY STRICT conditions FOR OLIVIA

① NO being annoying.

That's it. As soon as she starts to be annoying she has to go back to her own room.

NO COMEBACKS OR QUESTIONS ASKED OR ANSWERED.

I even drew up a contract and made her sign it in front of me and Bob.

CONTRACT

Sign HERE

BoB

I, Olivia, do solemnly promise (cross my heart hope to die) my beautiful, adorable and talented sister, Ella, that I will NOT under ANY CIRCUMSTANCES annoy ANY of her friends (especially Zoe) at ANY time during the duration of the CUUC sleepover on pain of being asked to leave immediately and sent to my room with only ONE (1) small snack of Ella's choice.

Signed: Witness:

X Olivia X 🐾

Zoe and I called our friends this afternoon and they can all make it.

I CAN'T WAIT until tomorrow night!

G'night, Diary, sweet dreams.

xoxo

Saturday afternoon, after lunch

Hey, Diary,

Dad and I spent the morning baking snacks and cutting up fruit for my sleepover. This is what we made:

1 Banana CAKE

2 chocolate crackles

3 APPLE and raisin MUFFINS

4 chocolate CHIP COOKIES

5

tropical · fruit
PLATTER

6 Plus one chocolate pizza. (Ha-ha—only kidding! But it sounds yummy though. ☺)

Have to go—the banana cake is ready to be iced with lemon and coconut frosting.

De-lish!

LEMON   coconut

xxx

Saturday, late afternoon

Can't write much now, Diary. I'm too busy organizing everything for the ~~Sleepover of the Century~~ Millennium! This is what I've put together so far:

♥ Snacks and drinks ☑

♥ Cassi Valentine songs (loaded on my MP3 player) ☑

♥ Cassi Valentine live concert DVD ☑

♥ Extra pillows, cushions, blankets and throws (sleepover guests are bringing their own sleeping bags) ☑

♥ Scrap paper and glitter pens to scribble down ideas ☑

♥ Mom's whiteboard and **mark**

Ooooo—there goes the doorbell now!

CYA!

Sunday night, in bed (yawn . . .)

Dearest, darlingest Diary,

I am ~~EXHAUSTERATED~~ EXHAUSTED.

The sleepover was (mostly) aMAZing!
First of all we watched the Cassi Valentine
DVD. Twice. While it was playing we made
up our own crazy dance routines to her
songs. Zoe's and mine was the best.
Then we took turns to sing one of
her songs in front of a judging panel
like we were doing auditions
for a reality TV talent show.

Daisy, Chloe and Georgia won golden tickets to go straight to

CASSI-WOOD

(Cassi-wood is kind of like Hollywood, only with better songs and outfits.)

We had Blindfolded

Makeovers

and a chocolate chip cookie-eating
competition
(Guess who won?
Hint: Her name rhymes
with "stellar")

and a kooky fashion parade

and handstand competitions. Zoe lasted the longest (47 seconds).

Cordelia roamed around the room taking random photos of everyone with her dad's ancient old Polaroid camera he used to have when he was a boy (during the Dark Ages). We made a big display of all her pictures.

LOOK 👁
in
HeRe!

PoLaroid
cAMERA

Finally we got down to business.

We put all of the snacks
on a big tablecloth on the
floor to allow for maximum
reachability. And I turned
down my MP3 player (just
a little bit—we still wanted
to hear Cassi singing!) so
we could hear each other talking. Then we
started brainstorming ideas for the CVVC
on the whiteboard.

Here's what we came up with:

iDEAS for the CVVC ♡ Meeting

IDEA	Why it would be good	Why it wouldn't be
① Film the whole school singing one of Cassi's songs, even the littlies and the boring boys (and Fiona).	It would show Cassi (and the judges) that we believe that everyone should be allowed to have a turn (even if they're not actually very good or only like bagpipe music). Judges LOVE stuff like that.	Some kids have really bad or squeaky voices or would mess around and spoil it for everyone else. Or both.

IDEA	Why it would be good	Why it wouldn't be
② Film only the really good singers (like Zoe and me and Georgia and Chloe—OK, and Poppy and Daisy too—OK, AND OLIVIA!!) singing one of Cassi's songs.	When Cassi sees how good we are, not only will we win the competition, she might invite us to tour with her as her backup singers.	~~No reasons.~~ Maybe Cassi will just think we're copying her songs (which anyone with even a tiny brain could do) and it would be better if we came up with original stuff.

3 Lock Peach in a cupboard so she misses the meeting.	The look on her face!!!	She'd probably turn us in to Ms. Weiss or (worse) Mr. Martini (the principal) and we would be put in detention FOR-EVER.
4 I could write a new song for Cassi and we could film me singing it.	Cassi's record company might sign me up for a songwriting deal!	It wouldn't be dumb at all. It would be fabulously fabulous!

And then we had a vote.

Nobody voted for my idea (Number 4) which made me feel a bit sad, especially after what Mr. Zugaro said about my sensitive and artistic poem about the shivering sparrow. Not even Zoe, who's supposed to be my BFF. ☹

It's so not fair. I would have voted for her idea if she'd had one, even if I thought it was terrible. That's what best friends do for each other.

BFF

ZOE!

Number 3 (locking Peach in a cupboard) got the most votes. It was Georgia's idea. It is ~~ackshert~~ actually a really excellent idea (though not as good as mine). The kind of idea master spies that work for top secret secret agencies might think up.

LOCK PEACH inside

Princess Peach is ALWAYS trying to ruin everyone's plans and make their life ~~miserarumble~~ miserable. If she is locked in a cupboard she won't be able to be Miss Perfect Big Shot at the meeting and trick the teachers into choosing her ideas. YES!!!

So, it was all settled. I put a big tick next to Number 3 and started another section on the whiteboard: OPERATION PEACH CUPBOARD SNATCH so we could plan how we were going to do it.

And then Olivia started blubbing like a BIG BABY because she was worried about getting in trouble with the teachers. And then Georgia and Chloe and Daisy started looking at Olivia and then over at me and rolling their eyes, like they were thinking, "who invited HER?"

And then Poppy said she wouldn't do Number 3 either

for the same reasons. And then Georgia told her to GROW UP and stop being such a Scaredy Cat from Ballarat.

And Poppy said that was so not true, because she didn't even live in Ballarat. And then she threw a chocolate crackle cupcake at Georgia.

Georgia

So Georgia threw an apple and raisin muffin back.

And everyone else started yelling, "FOOD FIGHT! FOOD FIGHT!" and throwing gooey snacks and squashy fruit at each other.

My sensational sleepover had suddenly turned into a BIG MESS. There was lemon frosting all over the sofa and bits of squashed grape and watermelon all over the carpet. This was MUCH worse than the Krazee Kolor Hair Color Disaster. I kept waiting for Mom and Dad to storm into our sleepover and SHUT IT ALL DOWN.

And then something really FREAKY and STRANGE happened. Cordelia started jumping up and down like she had an armadillo in her pillow, screaming, "Guess what? I've just had a really EXCELLENT idea!"

And everyone stopped throwing gooey snacks and/or blubbing and turned around and stared at her.

Cordelia is usually really, really quiet. She hardly ever speaks. (Unless she's talking to her favorite furry friend, Mr. Wombat.) She DEFINITELY doesn't scream.

cordelia

 So we all listened very carefully to what she had to say.

Bet you want to know what it was, don't you? I'd tell you, but I'm too tired to keep writing right now.

Don't worry, you'll get to hear the rest of it tomorrow. Cordelia's idea is BRILLIANT. We are going to win that competition for sure.

G'night, Diary Doo.
Sweet dreams.
Hope that mine come true.
xxx

Monday, straight after school

Dear Diary,

I am shocked. **SHOCKED!**

Just when I thought everything was going really, really well, Precious Princess Peach Parker has to spoil everything. AGAIN!

Precious
PEACH Parker

Grrrrr! We so should have locked her in that cupboard. ☹

Here's what happened at the meeting.

About twenty kids turned up. Peach and her buddies Prinny and Jade tried to sit right up in front of course, so they could get maximum sucking-up points. But Ms. Weiss said she wanted everyone to sit in a circle so that we were all "equal."

Ha!

Then Ms. Weiss asked us all "to share" our ideas with her and Mr. Zugaro.

And guess what? Most of the other kids'
ideas were EXACTLY the same as our
Number 1 and Number 2 from the sleepover
meeting.

YAWN.

I was just about to tell everyone Cordelia's
Brilliant Idea (because she was too shy to
do it herself) when
Princess Peach
bulldozed right over
the top of me and
said in her super-
fakey voice:

Peach
Parker!

ME!

"Oooo, Ms. Weiss, I'm just SOOO excited about my idea I can't wait ANY LONGER. Ple-e-e-ase can I go next? If I don't tell you right now, I'm going to BURST!"

Ms. Weiss and Mr. Zugaro traded one of those looks that says "Isn't she adorable?"

BLEUChhh!!

Why can't they see that she's just a Big. Fat. Fake?

And then Mr. Zugaro laughed a little laugh and said, "Sure, Peach. We don't want you bursting, do we, Ms. Weiss?"

And Ms. Weiss shook her head and said, "No, we certainly can't let that happen," like Peach was her favorite student. Which is so not fair. I always thought I was her favorite student. ☹

So then Peach did her shark smile again. And then she said making a video of a whole lot of kids (even talented ones like her and her friends Prinny and Jade) singing one of Cassi's songs would be too BORING and OBVIOUS to win the competition. And that probably ALL the other schools were going to do that too. So it was up to OUR school to do something COMPLETELY DIFFERENT.

"Good point," said Mr. Zugaro, utterly mesmerized* by her shark smile.

Mr. Zugaro

shark SMILE

✳ Mesmerized means being sucked in
by something. Just like those singing
mermaids used to do to sailors in the
olden days, before they wrapped them up in
their ratty old seaweedy mermaid hair and
drowned them at the bottom of the sea
with all the other rotting sailors and stinky
dead sea creatures. Eww.

singing
Mermaid

Peach's smile got bigger and sharkier. "So, why don't we show the things we're good at here in our school?" she said. "You know, stuff like the big band, and the rock band, and the singing club, and the girls that do gymnastics in the gym with me at lunchtime. And we'd all be playing or singing or dancing our OWN stuff. Not just Cassi's."

I couldn't believe it. That was OUR idea.
Exactly. The one Cordelia had told us at
the sleepover. And now Peach was trying to
make out like it was hers.

NOOOOOOOOOOOOOOO!

It couldn't be happening AGAIN! Could it?
How DARE she!

Why, Diary? Why?

How did she do it? How did she find out?

All of these important questions and more
kept looping around and around in my brain,

like a barrel of rattlesnakes with their tails in their mouths.

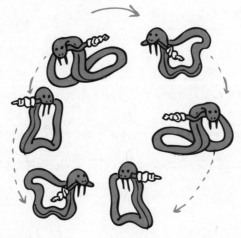

Have to stop now, Diary. I'm too wounded to keep writing.

I may never recover.

Yours in pain,
Ella

Monday night, in bed

Back again, Diary.

I'm feeling a little bit stronger now after
a soothing cup of hot chocolate. (Nanna Kate
always says a nice strong cup of tea is
the bees' knees* when you are having a
crisis, but I had a sip of
hers one time and it was
disGUSTing. Eww.)

HOT → I ♥ Chocolate

* I am not 100% sure
that bees actually have knees and even if
they did, how could their sting-y old knees
make you feel better?

So I'm going to try to write more about what happened next at the meeting. WARNING: Some of this might make you REALLY upset and/or angry.

After Peach had finished telling Ms. Weiss and Mr. Zugaro her (OUR!!) brilliant idea and Ms. Weiss and Mr. Zugaro had finished telling Peach how totally fabulous it was, she sat down again with this big sucky teacher's pet smirk on her face.

That SMIRK!!

And then Mr. Zugaro said there was just enough time for one more idea before the bell rang.

I couldn't speak. I was too shocked. So I just sat there, like a sad little fly that has just been swatted by a gigantic flyswatter.

Gigantic flySWATTER

Zoe gave me a desperate "Come on, say something" look.

And I gave her a desperate "I can't, I'm too shocked" look back.

We sat there for about 900 hours, giving each other desperate looks.

900 HRS

And then finally Zoe gave me a really sharp shoving shove with her elbow so I stood up and said the first thing that came into my head.

"Um . . ."

Everyone in the circle stared at me, waiting to hear what I was going to say next. Especially Peach.

"Um . . . well . . . I could write a song. And then we can get the singing club to sing it. And the big band and the rock band and all the other bands to play different bits of the music for it."

I sneaked a look at Mr. Zugaro and Ms. Weiss. They weren't throwing up or holding their hands over their faces trying not to laugh, which was a good sign. In fact, they were nodding and smiling, so I kept going.

"And the girls that do gymnastics at lunchtime, they can be the backup dancers like all the big pop stars have, and . . . and . . ."

I stared wildly out the window like a wild thing, in case a good idea was sneakily lurking outside, waiting for me to discover it. I needed something BIG. Something SERIOUSLY SPECTACULAR and

SENSATIONAL that no one (especially Peach) could ever think up in a zillion gatrillion years.

And then I saw her. Walking around all by herself on the other side of the field (because everyone within hearing distance had run away) doing her music practice.

YESSSS! This was PERFECT!

Bagpipes.

FIONA

". . . and Fiona McTavish could play it on her bagpipes!" I said.

Then I sat down again, exhausted from all that idea thinking up.

Both Mr. Zugaro and Ms. Weiss absolutely, completely, totally, utterly, 100% ADORED my idea. I know this because they told me.

But then they said something terrifyingly terrible.

Something so horrifically horrifying I will probably die a tragic and heartbreaking death and never recover from it.

Something so alarmingly awful I can't bring myself to write it down, because that will make it real.

So long, dear Diary. Until we meet again . . .

Yours,
Ella

Tuesday morning, before school

Still can't write about it.

Tuesday, after school

Nope.

Tuesday, after dinner

Mr. Zugaro and Ms. Weiss said that . . .

Nope. Sorry, can't do it.

Tuesday night, very, very, very late

OK. Here it comes, ready or not.

Mr. Zugaro and Ms. Weiss said that they loved BOTH our ideas. Because they were refreshingly "fresh" and "original." And that we should . . . we should . . .

You know what's coming next, don't you?

They want Peach and me to work on the video project.

Together.

Wednesday, after school

Dear Diary,

Zoe and I discussed how I could get out of working with Peach on our way to school this morning.

WAY OF NOT WORKING WITH PEACH	WHY IT WON'T WORK
① Go to school disguised as a new student, with a different hairstyle, bushy eyebrows (drawn on with one of Max's brown crayons) and wearing Mom's reading glasses, so Ms. Weiss wouldn't recognize me.	It was too late for this one now because we were already on our way to school.

2 Kidnap Peach and lock her in the teachers' lounge, then put a sign on the door saying: NO ENTRY DUE TO DANGEROUS ~~CHEMICLE~~ CHEMICAL SPILLAGE. DO NOT ENTER ON PAIN OF DEATH THIS MEANS YOU (with a skull and crossbones symbol) so they wouldn't go in and find her.

Peach might escape out of the window or a teacher might accidentally go in without reading the sign because they left their reading glasses at home and Peach would escape and/or turn us in to them.

3 Tell Peach that Cassi Valentine had just been spotted hanging around Peach's house, so she'd rush home to see her and get into trouble for being out of school without a signed note from her parents and get kicked off the project.

Zoe thought this one up, but no way is Peach going to believe ANYTHING I ever tell her, ~~expesh~~ especially if it's something to do with Cassi Valentine.

Cassi Valentine

(LIMO)

It was then we realized it was all hopelessly hopeless, and I was going to have to work with Peach whether I liked it or not.

IT'S THIS ONE!

But zoe—like a TRUE FRIEND—said she would help me out if Peach got too annoying. (Which is a BIG RELIEF, because after she didn't vote for my idea at the sleepover I wasn't 100% sure we were BFFs anymore, which would be DEVASTATING, especially since we have been BFFFs.*)

ME   ZOE

* BFFFs = Best Friends Forever Forever.

So anyway, when lunchtime came, we had another meeting in the music room. Mr. Zugaro let us in and said he would "pop back later to see how we were doing." (Ha! Teachers always say that when what they really plan to do is go and sit in the comfy teachers' lounge and drink coffee and do the crossword and forget that you and your meeting ever ~~exited~~ existed.)

TEACHERS' LOUNGE

Most of the kids from the first meeting didn't turn up. Probably because their extremely boring and obvious ideas didn't get chosen. Which is just SO ~~immachewer~~ immature and babyish. But all my friends from the sleepover came. And of course You Know Who.

This is what happened.

Peach: OK, let's get started.
Me (outraged): Who made you the boss?
Peach (taking out an adorable and stylish Cassi Valentine-themed notebook and pen which she must have gotten her mom to buy her from Stationery"R"Us especially

for the meeting.
Why didn't I think of
that??): Mr. Zugaro
and Ms. Weiss did,
OK?
Me: No, it's not OK,
OK? They said we
have to work on the video

Cassi
Valentine-themed
NoteBook
(and pen!)

"together."

Georgia (yawning): So why don't you just
get on with it then.
Me: Yeah, Peach. Why don't you? And anyway,
you're not the boss of me.

Peach (wrinkling her nose as if there was a bad smell in the room): That's what you think.

Me: At least I can think. I don't just copy other people's good ideas all the time.

Peach (looking fake shocked): SOOO did not.

Me: SOOO did too.

FAKE!

Peach and I traded a few more insults as if we were playing Insult Ping-Pong. And then we just glared at each other with our arms folded across our fronts like the kids on the soccer team do in their team photo.

Then Zoe gave me one of her shoving shoves and hissed at me to stop arguing with Peach because all the other kids like Georgia and Poppy and even Prinny and

Jade were getting twitchy and were about to walk out.

Oops.

If everyone walked out there'd be no one to make the video. And if we didn't make the video, we wouldn't win the competition. And then I'd NEVER get to meet Cassi Valentine!

So I unfolded my arms and said, "OK, let's get started," which I thought was extremely ~~machewer~~ mature of me.

And Peach looked around with a big phony smile and said, "Fine with me," in this supersweet queenly voice.

Bleuchhh. She is such a  FAKE!

So then we wrote all the things that we needed for the video on the whiteboard and then everyone filled in their names under what they wanted to do.

OuR aMAZing CVVC pLaN

1 write the song for the video.

Ella

2 write a script for the video and find someone who is a good videoer to video it.

Zoe

3 Talk to the gymnastics girls and ~~tell~~ ask them to create a special dance.

Peach, Prinny and Jade

4 Talk to the singing club kids and ~~tel~~ ask them to sing.

Georgia and Chloe

5 Ask all the bands in the school to play.

Poppy and Daisy

6 Talk to Fiona McTavish about playing her bagpipes.

Bagpipes.

Things were going really well until we got to
Number 6. Nobody wanted to do that one.
And then Peach said it was my idea so I
had to do it. And I said no I didn't (in case
Fiona got overexcited and tried to give me
a special private bagpiping performance
and blew up my eardrums and all my
brains leaked out of my ears. Eww).

Like this.

So then we started glaring and arm folding again.

Everyone else started rolling their eyes and doing long sighs and saying stuff about walking out again. Even Zoe. ~~Acksherly~~ Actually, especially Zoe.

So then Cordelia (who was just sitting there watching quietly) said she would do it (even though you could tell she really didn't want to) and wrote her name on the board next to Number 6.

PHEW.

The last thing we wrote on the board was:

 Design costumes.

Anyone with even a tiny brain knows how
fabulously fabulously fabulous I am when
it comes to designer-ish things. I am
FAMOUS for being able to throw unrelated
clothing items together in a trendsettingly
and attractively super-stylish way.

frilly
Bathing Suit

Dad's
Barbecue
apron

LACE
Curtains

Nanna KATE'S
Velvet Slippers

So I was positively, definitely

expecting what happened next.

WHAT HAPPENED NEXT:

Every time I wrote my name next to Number 7, Peach crossed it out and wrote hers. So then I crossed hers out and wrote mine. And then she crossed mine out and wrote hers. We kept writing and crossing out until the board looked like this:

 **7** Design costumes.

And then I turned around and noticed something, just as Mr. Zugaro "popped back in" to see how we were getting on.

Everyone else had gone.

Including Zoe.

Have to go now, Diary. Will write more soon.
I promise.

Ella

Wednesday night, after dinner

Dear Diary,

I am supposed to be working on my song for the CVVC with Zoe, only she didn't come around after school and stay for dinner like we arranged with her mom this morning because she reckons she is not talking to me until I stop acting like a baby by having silly arguments with Peach all the time which is obviously NEVER in a gatrillion years to the power of a kazillion going to happen so I

guess Zoe and I aren't BFFs anymore, and ESPECIALLY not BFFFs.
Now I'm going to have to write the song all by myself.

Anyway, SO WHAT? WHO CARES? I can probably do a MUCH better job on my own.

I am going to start RIGHT NOW.

This is exciting! Wish me luck, Diary.

Wednesday night, about five minutes later

I wonder if there is any banana cake left in the fridge?

Wednesday night, about five minutes after that

Hmmm. Maybe Max and Bob would like me to read them a bedtime story . . . I'll just go and see.

Wednesday night, half an hour later

They did! And then I read them three more!

So I'm too tired for songwriting now, Diary.

Good night.

Thursday night, after dinner

I wonder if Olivia needs any help with her homework?

Thursday night, about twenty minutes after that

OK, enough time ~~wasterizing~~ wasting. I am going to start writing my song right now.

Here it comes.

I wonder if that scratching sound I can hear coming from the back door is Bob wanting to go outside to pee. I better just go and check.

Thursday night, about three minutes after that

Sorry. False alarm.

Right. I'm just going to change to my lucky pen. That should do the trick.

Thursday night, who cares what the time is?

Writing songs is REALLY, REALLY hard, Diary. Especially when you have to do it all by yourself. ☹

Most songs you hear on the radio just go like this:

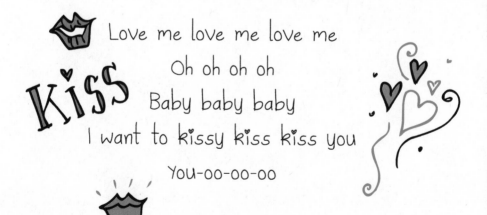

Love me love me love me
Oh oh oh oh
Baby baby baby
I want to kissy kiss kiss you
You-oo-oo-oo

Bleuchhh.

Anyone with even a tiny brain could write
something better than that. I am going
to stay up ALL NIGHT until I write a
really good song. That will show everyone.
Especially Peach (and Zoe).

Now I have TWO ex-BFFs. Do you think
that's some kind of record? ☹

Even later than the last time I wrote

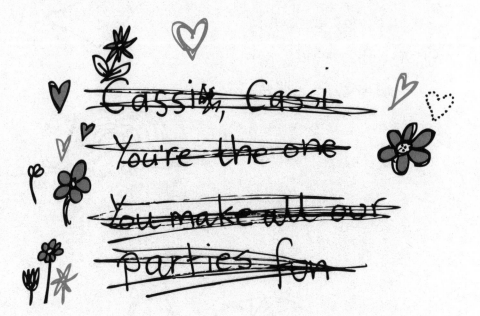

Oh no! I am
hopelessly hopeless
at songwriting. Mr.
Zugaro was probably
just being kind when
he told me my shivering
sparrow poem was a
masterpiece.

But if I don't write a song there will be nothing for the singing club to sing or the bands to play or the gymnastics girls to dance to or the videoer to video and we won't win the competition.

And then my dream to meet Cassi Valentine will just drift away like a drifty cloud in the breeze.

Nanna Kate reckons if you ever get stuck trying to do something you should think about it a lot from all different angles then "sleep on it." And then when you wake up in the morning, the answer will pop into your head, like a piece of toast popping out of a toaster.

So I'm going to try it right now, Diary.

Good night!

Friday morning, before school

Dearest Diary,

Guess what! Nanna Kate's advice worked!

When I woke up this morning there were words chasing each other around inside my head. I grabbed a piece of paper and scribbled them down before I forgot them.

My Head!

Ideas... ideas... ideas... ideas...

art
dance
music
creative
imagination
originality
vision
inspiration
dream
power
artistic
unique
beauty
truth

This is going to be the best song EVER!

I can't wait to show everyone on the CVVC committee.

But there's something really, really important I have to do first.

Bye!
Ella
XOXO

Friday, after school

Dearest Diary,

As soon as I got to school I looked around everywhere for Zoe. I finally found her in the girls' bathroom, talking to Georgia and Chloe.

ZOE

Me: Um . . . hey, Zoe.
Zoe (looking around and sniffing like someone had just stepped in dog poop): Did you hear something, Georgia?
Georgia: Nope. Did you, Chloe?
Chloe: Nope.

GEORGIA
Nope.
Nope.
Chloe

Me: I'm really sorry for arguing with Peach.
And I promise, cross my heart hope to die,
not to do it again.
Zoe: Too late.
Me: No way!
Zoe: Yes way. We don't even want to do the
video anymore.
Georgia: Yeah. We're out. And so are Poppy
and Daisy. You and Peach are going to have
to work "together" all by yourselves.
Me (panicking): But you can't. I've written
the song and EVERYTHING. It's really,
really good!
Zoe (turning to me, her eyes all shiny, and
sounding like the old Zoe again): You've
WRITTEN THE SONG!!?

Me (hoping it is good, even a little bit):
Yep. I stayed up practically ALL NIGHT!
Zoe (jumping up and down with excitement):
Why didn't you tell me? Have you got it
with you now? Quick! Show me!
Me (grabbing the song out of my backpack
and passing it to Zoe): ☺
Zoe (reading the song): Zow-ee, Ell. This
song is aMAZing! When can we start?
Me: ☺☺☺☺☺☺

Have to go now, Diary. Zoe's coming around for an Emergency Video Planning meeting.

It's going to be fabulously fabulous to the power of a megatrillion!

CYA later alligator,
E x

Wednesday, in bed, just before lights-out

My dearest Diary,

You must think I had ~~abbanderned~~ ~~abandorned~~ forgotten all about you! But I would NEVER do that. The last five days just whizzed past like a whirling whirlwind. So much exciting stuff has happened!

The good news

Our CVVC project is back on again!

The other good news

The singing club have all been buzzing away like busy buzzy little bees learning my song. Tra-la-la-ti-da! ♪♫♫♪♫

Shannon Mantell, who is in Grade 6 and a SERIOUSLY SERIOUS musician (she plays so many different musical instruments I do not have enough room on the page to write them all down and anyway some of them are REALLY hard to spell) wrote excellent music to go with it.

Peach and the other gymnastics girls are all madly practicing their high kicks and cartwheels and splits and pulling their hair back into ballet buns which are so tight their eyes nearly pop out of their heads. (Princess Peach has made herself the MAIN dancer of course.)

Everyone is just going to wear plain black leggings and either red or black T-shirts. (This was Zoe's idea, so Peach and I don't murder each other.)

And guess who Ms. Weiss chose to do the BIG introduction at the start?

HINT: Their name rhymes with "mortadella!" ☺

The good better news

Cordelia is going to shoot* the video, because she is good at taking pictures and doesn't get upset when you yell at her

to move closer/
get farther away/
zoom in NOW!!
like some other
people I know (not
naming names or
anything).

Video CAMERA

We are doing it tomorrow. YAY!!!

* This is the special word famous video
directors use when what they actually mean
is "video the video." So why don't they just
say that, instead of scaring everybody out
of their tiny brains so much they nearly
don't turn up?

The even better news!

Fiona McTavish accidentally left her bagpipes
on a bus by
accident and they
were never seen
(or heard) again.
Ever.

Bagpipes

Actually, this is not 100% true. Or even 1%
true. It is just a story I made up to make
myself feel better.

The puzzling and Bamboozling ✳ mysterious news

Peach wants to have a special secret meeting tomorrow before the video shoot. Just me and her.

I wonder what she wants to talk about? Maybe she's going to say sorry for all the times she's been mean to me. Yes. That must be it!

Who knows? Maybe we can even start to be BFFs again!

✳ My new favorite word!

Thursday, after school

I am shocked, Diary. SHOCKED! To the power of infinity!

Princess Peach didn't want to say sorry. She just wanted to get me all alone so she could lock me in a cupboard!

How DARE she!!

When I got to the meeting room, Prinny and Jade were waiting behind the door. They grabbed me and pushed me into the cupboard where Mrs. Fandango keeps all her fusty old music stuff that has been in there since the Jurassic Era. Eww.

But guess what?

Cordelia was in the girls' bathroom and she heard them all secretly whispering about what they were going to do. So she found Zoe and told her.

Zoe and Cordelia waited until they saw Peach leave. Then they came rushing to my rescue, like valiant knightesses* in shining armor!

* Knightesses are kind of like princesses, only they are much braver and ride around doing good deeds on really cool horses.

And guess what else?

I found out the reason Peach tried to lock me in the cupboard was so I wouldn't be there to sing my song, and then when no one could find me she was going to kindly offer to step in at the last moment and sing it instead. And then Cassi Valentine would think she was the star of the show.

MEANIE.

She hasn't changed ONE LITTLE BIT.

Anyway, all that drama made me feel a bit twitchy and emotional. So Zoe said I should just forget about doing the big introduction and save my strength for the main part of the video, where everyone dances around me while I sing my song.

So Mr. Wombat and Cordelia did the introduction instead and Ms. Weiss videoed this part. Cordelia didn't want to do it, because she's so shy, and said she would get too nervous and throw up. (Eww.) But then Zoe and I said to make it look like Mr. Wombat was doing the actual talking, so she tried that instead.

And guess what? They were senSATional!
(I think she ~~sekretly~~ secretly enjoyed it.)

MR. Wombat

Friday, after school

Dearest Diary,

Ms. Weiss sent our video off to the competition today.

Cross your fingers (and pages—ha-ha) and hope we win!

One week later

Waiting patiently to hear if we won . . .

Two weeks later

Still waiting . . .

Three weeks later

It is SO not fair. I am going to waste away
from waiting, like a sad, faded autumn leaf
at the end of a
long, lonely summer.
And nobody in my
family seems to
care . . .

waiting...

ME

waiting...

waiting....

Three and a half weeks later

The bad news

We didn't win.

But we came second! The judges  said our video was "fresh and original," which is EXACTLY what Mr. Zugaro and Ms. Weiss said about Peach's and my ideas.

Maybe if we hadn't argued so much, and worked together better, we could've come first. ☹☹☹☹☹

The good news

St. Finbar's (the school up
the road from us) won!

And their music teacher
Mr. Nova is VERY good friends with Ms.
Weiss. And he invited all the people who
were in the video (even Fiona McTavish—
which means he mustn't have very good
hearing) to come to their prize-winning
lunchtime concert. Which was today!!!

And guess what! You never will and I'm
DYING to tell you so don't even bother
guessing this time.

At the end of the concert the band stopped playing and the backup dancers stopped backup dancing and Cassi Valentine stood all alone in the middle of the stage.

Then she picked up her microphone and said, "I'd like to ask a VERY SPECIAL PERSON from the audience to join me here on stage. Someone who I think is a REAL STAR."

And then Princess Peach started smirking and flicking her hair like she thought SHE was the Very Special Person and the REAL STAR, because of all the high kicks and cartwheels and splits she'd done in the

video. She even got ready to stand up and
run down to the stage.

Cassi kept talking. "So I'd like her to
come down here to help me sing a VERY
SPECIAL SONG. It's called 'Dreams Come
True.'"

And guess whose name she called out?

Hint: The answer
rhymes with
"NINE!"

xx

Dreams Come True

Hey did you ever—
Dream a dream
Did you look into the sky at night
Where the bright stars gleam
Catch a rainbow
Chase a cloud
Dance with the breeze—
Or just follow the crowd?

You've got to follow your dream
Wherever it may lead
Follow your star
No matter how far

Just never give up
And never give in
If you follow your dream
You'll always win
Yes if you follow your dream
You'll always win.

ELLA Diaries

Read them all!